# There was a boy so disgusting they called him Yuck

# MATT AND DAVE

# YUCK

# YUCK'S AMAZING UNDERPANTS

## AND

# YUCK'S SCARY SPIDER

**Illustrated by Nigel Baines**

www.yuckweb.com

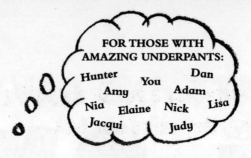

FOR THOSE WITH
AMAZING UNDERPANTS:
Hunter   You   Dan
   Amy      Adam
Nia   Elaine   Nick   Lisa
Jacqui      Judy

SIMON AND SCHUSTER

First published in Great Britain in 2007
by Simon & Schuster UK Ltd
A CBS COMPANY

Africa House 64–78 Kingsway London WC2B 6AH

3 5 7 9 10 8 6 4

A CIP catalogue record for this book is
available from the British Library

ISBN 978-1-8473-8194-1

Typeset by Nigel Baines
Printed and bound in Great Britain by
Cox & Wyman Ltd Reading Berkshire

www.simonsays.co.uk
www.yuckweb.com

# YUCK'S AMAZING UNDERPANTS

Yuck came downstairs to say goodnight.
He was dressed like a superhero, wearing
his underpants outside his pyjamas.

"Yuck, why are you dressed like that?"
Dad asked.

"These are my Amazing Underpants,"
Yuck said.

"They stink!" his sister Polly Princess told
him, pinching her nose.

Yuck's underpants were dirty and crusty
and smelly. He had been wearing them
every day and every night for six weeks.

"They're full of germs," Mum told him.
"Go and put them in the laundry basket
at once!"

Yuck ran out of the living room. He raced straight upstairs to his bedroom and hopped into bed.

From under his pillow he pulled out a torch and his Superspy Magnifying Glass. He dived under the covers to investigate.

Through the magnifying glass Yuck

could see hundreds of germs squirming and wiggling in his underpants.

They were almost ready!

Yuck reached over the side of his bed and shone his torch onto Swampland. He grabbed his jar of mould.

From his bedroom floor he picked up a paintbrush. It was one he'd borrowed from Polly's painting set. He dipped the paintbrush into the jar and stirred the green mould round and round.

"It's time for a midnight feast," he said, heading back under the duvet.

Yuck painted a thick blob of green mould onto his underpants, working it deep into the crusty cloth.

He painted another blob, then another. He dabbed mould all over his underpants, first on the outside and then again on the inside.

By the time he'd finished, his underpants were mouldy and green.

Yuck smiled. He lay down and closed his eyes, feeling the germs nibbling and wiggling, eating the mould as he drifted off to sleep.

In the morning, Yuck woke up giggling. Something was tickling him under the duvet. He threw back the covers and looked down.

Wow! His underpants were moving!

Yuck grabbed his Superspy Magnifying Glass and inspected them closely.

In the night, the germs had eaten the mould. They'd grown and multiplied. MILLIONS of them were crawling and wiggling in front of his eyes. His underpants were ALIVE with germs!

"Rockits!" Yuck said.

At that moment, his door opened.

Polly Princess came into his room.

"Get up, Yuck," she told him. "Mum says you've got to help with the cleaning!"

"CLEANING?" Yuck asked.

Mum came in behind Polly. "Your room is disgusting, Yuck," she said.

Mum started picking up the dirty underpants and socks from Yuck's floor.

"What about those ones?" Polly said, pointing to the underpants Yuck had on over his pyjamas.

"No!" Yuck shouted. "You can't wash these!"

"I told you to put those in the laundry basket," Mum said. She pulled Yuck's underpants off his legs.

"But they're my—"

"Don't be silly, Yuck," Mum told him.

"They're dirty and crusty and smelly," Polly said.

"Now get dressed and come and help with the cleaning," Mum said.

She carried Yuck's underpants out with the rest of the dirty washing. Polly stuck her tongue out, then ran downstairs.

Yuck decided that when he was
EMPEROR OF EVERYTHING,
everyone's underpants would be dirty.
It would be the LAW. Anyone who tried to
clean their underpants would be bounced
up and down in the WEDGIE MACHINE
and fired into the HAIRY HOLE.

Yuck got up and put his clothes on. He emptied the mould from his jar into his trouser pocket then crept to the bathroom.

He grabbed his mouldy underpants from the laundry basket, stuffed them up his T-shirt and ran downstairs.

Mum was wiping the kitchen table.

Dad was scrubbing the kitchen floor.

Polly picked up a pink feather duster and went to dust the living room.

Yuck followed her.

He sneaked in and hid behind the sofa.

Polly dusted the ornaments.

She dusted the pictures on the walls.

Then she dusted the trophy she'd won in a colouring competition.

She stood back to admire her work. Everything looked shiny and clean.

"Mum! I've finished!" she called.

While Polly went to fetch Mum, Yuck crept out from behind the sofa.

"Let's help her," he whispered to his underpants. Yuck dipped them into his pocket of mould, and they started wriggling in his hand.

He put them onto the mantelpiece, and they wriggled over the ornaments. He wiped them up the wall, and they wriggled over the pictures. He put them on Polly's trophy and they wriggled up and down the shiny silver.

They covered everything in mould.

Yuck heard Polly coming back with Mum. He grabbed his underpants and hid behind the sofa.

The door opened.

"Polly, what have you done?" Mum asked. "It's filthy in here!"

"It was clean a minute ago," Polly said.

"What a mess you've made, Polly!" Mum snatched the pink feather duster.

"But it wasn't me!" Polly said, looking at the mess in the living room.

"Where's Yuck?" she asked.

Yuck kept very quiet.

"I thought he was helping you," Mum said.

Polly stormed out of the door.

While Mum cleaned up, Yuck sneaked out from behind the sofa. He crept to the coat rack in the hallway, and watched as Polly took the vacuum cleaner out of the cupboard under the stairs. She connected the long tube and switched it on.

The vacuum cleaner began sucking up dust and dirt from the carpet.

"Let's help her," Yuck whispered to his underpants. He dipped them into his pocket of mould and they wriggled in his hand. The more mould he gave them, the more they wriggled. They were growing stronger.

Yuck placed them on the floor and they crawled out from behind the coats.

As Polly pushed the vacuum cleaner, Yuck's underpants shot straight up the tube.

The vacuum cleaner groaned.

Polly gave it a kick.

The vacuum cleaner growled.

She looked down the tube to see what was blocking it.

## BANG!

Dust and dirt shot out of the end of the tube, covering Polly in a thick grey cloud.

Yuck giggled. He reached out from behind the coats and grabbed his underpants from the floor.

"Polly! What have you done now?" Mum shouted, running to see what had happened. The hallway was covered in dust. "What a mess you've made, Polly!"

Mum snatched the vacuum cleaner.

"But it wasn't me," Polly said, looking at the mess in the hallway.

"Where's Yuck?" she asked.

Yuck kept very quiet.

"I thought he was helping you," Mum said.

Polly stormed off into the kitchen.

She filled a bucket with soapy water. Then she grabbed a sponge and a rag, and went out of the front door to wash the car.

When Mum's back was turned, Yuck sneaked out from behind the coats and followed Polly outside.

Hiding behind the dustbin, he watched as Polly covered the car with foam and bubbles.

She rubbed it all over. Then she rinsed
the bubbles off and started polishing the car
with a rag.

Polly stood back to admire her work.

The car looked shiny and clean.

"Dad! I've finished!" she called.

While Polly went to fetch Dad, Yuck
crept out from behind the dustbin.

"Let's help her," he whispered to his
underpants.

He dipped them into his pocket of
mould, then for extra energy he dunked
them in the drain.

They lapped up the stinky brown water
and started wriggling.

They jumped out of Yuck's hands and onto the bonnet of the car. They were growing even stronger.

They crawled across the roof and up and down the doors.

They rubbed mould round and round the wheels and sloshed stinky brown water over the windscreen.

Yuck heard Polly coming back with Dad. He grabbed his underpants and hid behind the dustbin.

Dad looked at the car. "Polly! It's filthy!" he said.

"It was clean a minute ago," she told him.

"What a mess you've made, Polly!"

Dad snatched the rag.

"But it wasn't me!" Polly said, looking at the mess on the car.

"Where's Yuck?" she asked.

Yuck kept very quiet.

"I thought he was helping you," Dad said.

Polly stormed off through the side gate into the back garden.

Yuck followed her and hid in the bushes.

Polly fetched a broom and began sweeping the back path.

"Let's help her," Yuck said.

He filled his underpants with big balls of sticky mud. They seemed to like mud.

They wriggled and squelched, then jumped out of his hands, rustling in the bushes like an animal.

Yuck made a gap in the leaves and his underpants hopped into position.

He stretched them like a catapult.

PING!

# SPLAT!

His underpants shot sticky mud all over the kitchen window.

"Polly!" Mum shouted out. "What do you think you're doing?"

Polly turned and saw the window covered in mud.

"What a mess you've made, Polly!"

"But it wasn't me!" Polly said, looking at the mess on the window.

"Where's Yuck?" she asked.

Yuck came walking up the garden.

"Where have you been?" Mum asked.

"I've been helping Polly," Yuck said.

Polly glared at him.

"No, he hasn't," she said. "He hasn't done anything all morning."

"Come indoors now, both of you," Mum told them. "It's lunchtime."

Yuck and Polly went inside.

All through lunch
Yuck hid his
underpants under
the table, feeding
them mould from
his pocket.

"This afternoon, I'd like you both to tidy
your rooms," Mum said.

When Yuck and Polly had finished
eating, Mum cleared the table.

Yuck ran upstairs and lay on his bed
with his underpants.

"I think we deserve
a rest," he said, opening
his copy of *OINK*.

# PLANET OF THE UNDERPANTS

SPACEMONKEY LOOKED OUT
FROM HIS TIME MACHINE...

*1000*

IT WAS
1,000 YEARS
IN THE FUTURE

THERE WAS NO TRACE OF HUMAN LIFE.
ONLY UNDERPANTS HAD SURVIVED.

UNDERPANTS FLEW THROUGH THE AIR

THEY RACED THROUGH THE STREETS

THEY TOLD EACH OTHER JOKES...

Meanwhile, Polly was hard at work, tidying her room.

She put her clothes and toys away. She organized her books on the shelves. She ordered her pens by colour, polished her mirror and puffed up her pillows. She started making her bed.

Yuck put down his copy of *OINK*.

He sniffed. There was a tasty smell coming from downstairs. "Do you like chocolate?" he said to his underpants.

He picked them up and crept to the kitchen.

Mum had been baking. She was filling a cake tin with chocolate brownies.

Yuck crept up behind her and hid his

underpants in the mixing bowl on the counter.

Mum turned around. "What are you doing, Yuck?" she said.

"You're meant to be tidying your room."

"I've already done it," Yuck told her.

"That was very quick," Mum said.

While Mum was talking, Yuck's underpants wriggled in the mixing bowl. They were eating the leftover chocolate.

"I've been working very hard," Yuck said.

He watched as his underpants crawled from the bowl and lifted the lid of the cake tin. They jumped in and loaded themselves up with chocolate brownies.

"Can I go outside and play now, please?" Yuck asked.

"Off you go, then," Mum told him.

"Rockits!" Yuck said.

His underpants pressed the lid back on the cake tin and waddled behind the toaster.

While Mum put the cake tin in the cupboard, Yuck grabbed his underpants and ran outside.

They were full of chocolate brownies!

He carried them to the bottom of the garden.

"Good boy," Yuck said, dividing the chocolate brownies into two piles, one for his underpants and the other for himself.

Yuck's underpants seemed to like chocolate very much. They gobbled the brownies in seconds, then began hopping up and down.

They raced around the garden.

"Wow!" Yuck said.

His underpants could run!

Yuck picked up a tennis ball from the lawn. "Can you fetch?" he said.

Yuck threw the ball across the garden and his underpants chased after it.

They jumped on the ball, scooped it up and carried it back to him.

"Well done!" Yuck said, as they dropped the ball on the grass.

He gave them a pat, then picked up a Frisbee. "Can you catch?" he said.

He threw the Frisbee across the garden. His underpants chased after it, then leapt up and caught it in mid-air.

"Well done!" Yuck said.

Just then, the corners of his underpants pricked up as the next-door neighbours' dog started barking.

"Do you want to go and play?" Yuck asked.

His underpants ran off and burrowed under the garden fence.

The next-door neighbours' dog was doing a poo.

Yuck's underpants scurried to the dog poo, jumped in it and gobbled it up.

The underpants looked up and saw a squirrel, running up a tree. They chased after it, climbing up the tree trunk and jumping from branch to branch.

A little bird saw them, flapped its wings and took off.

Yuck's underpants started flapping too.

"Wow!" Yuck said.

His Amazing Underpants jumped off the branch and soared into the sky.

They could fly!

"Go, underpants, go!" Yuck called.

At that moment, Polly came outside. She'd finished tidying her room.

"Yuck!" she called. "Mum says you've got to come in now."

Yuck's underpants hovered above Polly's head.

"It's dinnertime," Polly called.

Yuck whistled, and his underpants dropped.

Polly screamed as they landed on her.

Mum came running out to see what had happened. "What on earth's the matter?" she asked.

"It's Yuck's stinky underpants!" Polly cried, pulling them off her head. "He threw them at me!"

Polly chucked them on the ground, and ran inside to wipe her face.

Yuck came walking up the garden.

"Put those in the laundry basket right now!" Mum told him.

"But, Mum, they're my—"

"Don't be silly, Yuck," Mum said. "Now do as you're told."

Yuck picked up his underpants, ran indoors and up the stairs.

Polly's bedroom door was open.

He peered in.

Her room was tidy.

He put his underpants on her bed.

"Wait here," Yuck said to them. "I won't be long. Have as much fun as you like."

He went back downstairs for dinner. Mum, Dad and Polly were sitting at the table eating. Polly was looking very pleased with herself.

"Polly's tidied her room," Dad told him.

"So have I," Yuck said, sitting down.

"He's lying," Polly said. "He hasn't done anything all day!"

"I'll be inspecting your rooms after dinner," Mum told them both.

Polly smiled at Yuck.

Yuck pushed his chicken pie around his plate.

"Eat up," Dad told him.

"I'm not hungry," Yuck said.

"Come on, Yuck. If you don't eat your dinner, you can't have a chocolate brownie," Mum said.

Polly's plate was clean. She'd eaten all her chicken pie. "Can I have a brownie, please, Mum?" she asked.

Mum stood up and fetched the cake tin from the cupboard.

It was empty!

"Who's stolen the chocolate brownies?" Mum demanded.

Everyone looked at Yuck.

"It wasn't me," Yuck said. "I've been cleaning and tidying."

Mum went to inspect his room.

Yuck jumped up and raced after her. Polly followed him.

As Mum opened Yuck's bedroom door, she coughed. "It's disgusting in here!"

"But that's the way I like it," Yuck said.

"You haven't tidied at all," Mum told him.

Suddenly there came a scream from Polly's room.

Mum ran to see what had happened.

Polly was standing in her doorway, shaking.

Her clothes and toys were scattered over the floor. Her books had fallen off the shelves. The lids were off her pens and ink was leaking on the carpet. Her pillows were torn and there were feathers everywhere. Her mirror was smeared with green mould, and her duvet was brown with chocolate.

"Polly!" Mum said. "It's filthy in here!"

"It was clean when I left it," Polly said.

"What a mess you've made!"

"But it wasn't me," Polly said.

Just then, she saw Yuck's underpants lying on her pillow.

"What are they doing in here?" she asked.

Yuck's underpants had been playing.
Mum picked them up.

"Yuck!" she shouted.

Yuck was giggling
in his room.

Mum took his
underpants to the
bathroom.

When she came
out, Yuck crept in and
grabbed them from the
laundry basket.

"Well done!" he said.

But as he turned to leave, Mum and
Polly were standing in the doorway.

"Not so fast!" Mum said.

"I told you he's been up to something,
Mum."

"Put those underpants back, Yuck!" Mum
told him.

"But Mum, they're my—"

"Don't be silly," Mum said. She grabbed
them and stuffed them back in the basket.

And when it was bedtime, Mum locked Yuck in his bedroom to make sure that he didn't take them out again.

She turned the key. "First thing in the morning, your underpants are going in the wash," she said.

"They're going to GET IT," Polly whispered at the door.

Yuck rattled the door handle.

"If Mum washes them, they'll DIE," he said.

That night, Yuck dreamed he was the only soldier at Fort Underpants. He was surrounded by washing machines, attacking him from all sides, bombarding him with bubbles. Then, all of a sudden, he heard the call of a trumpet. From a faraway hill he saw hundreds of underpants riding towards him on horses. The cavalry were coming to save him!

In the morning, Yuck woke up and jumped straight out of bed. He banged on the door for someone to let him out.

The key turned. It was Polly. "You're too late," she said, grinning.

Yuck ran to the bathroom. The laundry basket had gone.

He ran downstairs and burst into the kitchen. The washing machine was spinning. The clothes were whirring round and round.

"No!" Yuck shouted.

Dad was sitting at the table reading the newspaper. "What's the matter, Yuck?" he asked.

"My Amazing Underpants are DEAD!" Yuck said.

The washing machine stopped and Mum pulled out the clothes.

Yuck could see lots of pairs of underpants, and all of them were CLEAN.

Polly came into the kitchen and stuck her tongue out at Yuck.

"I'll hang out the washing for you, Mum," she said.

"Good girl, Polly."

Dad put his newspaper down. "What do you mean, your underpants are dead, Yuck?" he asked.

Yuck looked at the newspaper on the table. He read the headline on the front page: UFO SPOTTED IN THE NIGHT.

Beneath it was a picture of something flying in the sky – something shaped like a pair of underpants.

Yuck ran out of the kitchen.

He raced upstairs to the bathroom. Looking closely, he could see a trail of green mould from the floor to the window.

The window was open.

Yuck ran to his room and opened his curtains. There, waiting for him outside, were his Amazing Underpants!

They saw him and started flapping.

"You escaped!" Yuck said. "You're alive!"

They were mouldy and muddy and covered in chocolate.

Yuck opened his window and gave them a great big hug.

"I'll NEVER let them clean you," he said. "You're the best underpants in the whole wide world."

Then he looked down.

In the garden, Polly was pegging the washing on the line to dry. Her basket was full of clean underpants.

"Let's help her," Yuck said.

He waited until Polly had gone back indoors, then released his underpants into the air. They flapped and circled high above the garden.

"Now!" he called.

His underpants
swooped down and
landed on the washing
line. They crawled along
it, stopping at each peg.
Whenever they passed a
pair of underpants, they
wriggled and shook,
sprinkling a shower of germs.

"Good boy," Yuck called.

He watched as all the underpants on
the line began twitching. Then he whistled
and his Amazing Underpants flapped and
took off.

"More!" Yuck called, pointing to the next-door neighbours' washing line.

His underpants flew across to next-door's washing and covered it in germs. Then they flew to the washing line in the next garden, and then the next. On every washing line in the neighbourhood, Yuck could see underpants starting to twitch.

He giggled. This was going to be fun.

He waited until all the underpants were ready.

"I think the washing's dry," he called down the stairs.

"I'll bring it in, Mum," Polly said.

She carried the empty basket outside, and started unpegging the washing from the line.

But something was wrong.

"Mum!" she called. "All the underpants have gone!"

At that moment, the sky turned dark as a big black cloud passed across the sun.

Polly looked up.

The big black cloud began flapping.

"Mum!" she called. "Help!"

Flying above her was a huge flock of underpants!

The sky was FULL of them! Dirty, crusty, smelly underpants!

Polly turned to run.

The underpants dived.

Pair after pair landed on her, hundreds of them, covering her in germs.

"Get them off me!" Polly shrieked. "Get them off me!"

Mum ran out to see what was happening. The garden was covered with washing. There were underpants everywhere. Polly was rolling on the ground.

"Polly! What have you done?"

"It wasn't me!" Polly screamed.

Underpants were crawling all over her. Germs were wriggling in her hair and her clothes.

Dad ran out from the kitchen. "Polly, what a mess you've made!" he said.

"It wa—" Polly's mouth was full of underpants.

At that moment,
Yuck whistled from
his bedroom window.

The dirtiest,
crustiest, smelliest pair
of underpants crawled
off Polly's head.

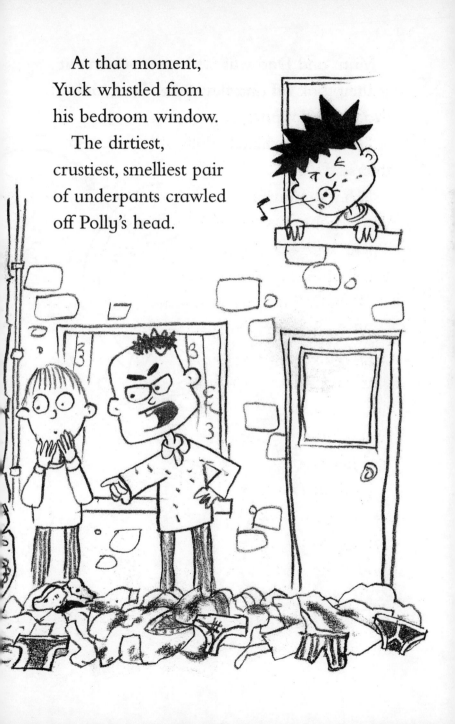

Mum and Dad watched in astonishment as they took off and flew up to Yuck, doing a loop-the-loop.

"That's incredible!"
Dad said.

"That's amazing!"
Mum said.

Yuck was laughing.

"I told you," he said. "They're my
Amazing Underpants!"

# YUCK'S SCARY SPIDER

Yuck and his sister, Polly Princess, were sitting at the kitchen table eating their breakfast. A big, fat, hairy scary spider came crawling under the back door.

Yuck smiled.

"What are you smiling at?" Polly asked him.

The spider scurried across the kitchen floor and disappeared under Polly's chair.

"Nothing," Yuck said, giggling.

"What's so funny?" Polly said.

Yuck pretended to drop his spoon. He bent down under the table and saw the spider climbing onto Polly's shoe. It crawled over her laces and crept up her sock.

Polly scratched her ankle. She could feel something tickling her.

The spider ran inside her trousers and up her leg.

"Aaaggghhh!" she screamed, jumping off her chair.

Yuck was laughing.

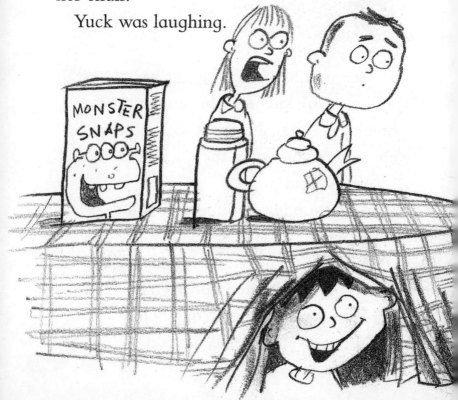

Polly shook her leg. "A spider! There's a spider in my trousers."

Mum and Dad came dashing in.

"What's going on in here?" Mum asked.

"A spider!" Polly screamed. "A big, fat, hairy, scary spider!"

The spider dropped out of Polly's trousers and scurried across the floor.

"Where did it go?" Dad asked, hunting under her chair.

Mum searched in the cupboards and behind the toaster. "It's gone," she said.

Just then, something big, fat and hairy tickled the top of Mum's head.

Yuck giggled.

The spider was hanging on a thread from the ceiling, crawling in Mum's hair.

"Uurrgghh!" Mum shouted.

"Quick, get it!" Polly screamed.

"It's only trying to be friendly," Yuck told them.

The spider dropped on to the floor.

"Squash it," Polly screamed, stamping her foot.

But the spider was much too quick for her. One second it was there, and the next it had gone.

"You scared it, Polly," Yuck told her.

"I hate spiders," Polly said, and she ran out of the kitchen.

Yuck got down on his hands and knees and started searching for the spider.

He couldn't find it anywhere.

"Hurry up or you'll be late for school," Mum said, handing him his bag.

When Yuck arrived at class, he raced to his seat next to Little Eric. "I saw a spider," he whispered.

Mrs Wagon the Dragon was standing at the front of the classroom.

"No talking, Yuck!" she said. "This week is Reading Week! I want you all to follow me to the library!"

Everyone stood up and followed the
Dragon out into the corridor.

"It was a big, fat, hairy scary
spider," Yuck whispered.

"Did you touch it?" Little Eric asked.

The Dragon opened the library door.

"I want each of you to choose a book,"
she said. "Then find a seat and read
quietly."

The school library
was full of row upon
row of books on
every subject.

"Can we choose any book we want, Miss?" Schoolie Julie asked.

"As long as it's not a picture book," the Dragon said. "And make sure you read it from cover to cover."

Yuck and Little Eric looked along the bookshelves.

SHHH!! QUIET!

Each bookshelf was marked with a letter.

A: Aliens... Arithmetic... Art...

B: Balloons... Banjos... Basketball...

C: Cats... Computers... Cookery...

Yuck ran to the shelf marked S. He read along the titles and took down a little yellow book. "*SPIDERS*," he read, showing it to Little Eric.

They took the book to a table in the far corner and sat down to read it together...

# SPIDERS

Spiders have eight legs and up to eight eyes. In the dark, they use hairs on their bodies to feel where they're going.

Spiders spin webs made of silk thread that is twice as strong as steel.

Spiders eat insects, and some even chomp mice and birds.

Some spiders have a poisonous bite, but only a few are harmful to humans. For safety, ask what type of spider it is before touching it.

As they were reading, Little Eric noticed something crawling out of Yuck's bag.

"Look!" he said, pointing.

Yuck looked. It was the big, fat, hairy scary spider!

"So THAT'S where it went!" Yuck said.

The spider crawled out of his bag and up the table leg.

"Is it poisonous?" Little Eric asked.

Yuck looked in his *SPIDERS* book. He pointed to a picture.

## THE SCARY SPIDER
Scientific name: Spidercus Scaricus
Description: Big, fat and hairy

Yuck read what it said in the book...

The Scary Spider is often mistaken
for the Poisonous Man-eating Spider,
Spidercus Horribilus, because of its
scary appearance. However, this is
a mistake. The Scary Spider is
non-poisonous and very friendly.
It is only hairy because it likes
to be cuddled.

"It's friendly," Yuck said.

He gave the spider a stroke. "You're not really scary, are you? You're a nice spider."

The spider tickled Yuck's finger with its hairy leg.

Yuck decided that when he was
EMPEROR OF EVERYTHING, he
would appoint himself Lord Protector of
Spiders. He'd live in a castle full of cobwebs
and flies. Spiders would come from miles
around to eat fly pie and sleep in
hammocks made of silk. Anyone who was
nasty to spiders would be squashed by THE
GIANT FOOT.

At lunchtime, Yuck and Little Eric stood in the queue for the canteen.

Frank the Tank and Clip-Clop Chloe were in front of them.

Yuck took the scary spider from his pocket and placed it on the counter by the knives and forks.

"A spider!" Frank the Tank screamed, running away.

"A scary spider!" Clip-Clop Chloe screamed, running after him.

"It's only trying to be friendly," Yuck called, picking the spider up.

Yuck and Little Eric took the last two burgers and sat down.

Yuck put the spider on his tray. While he ate his food, it scurried off to explore.

Polly Princess and Juicy Lucy were sitting at the table next to the teachers.

The spider scurried towards them.

"I've read two books today," Lucy said.

"I've read three," Polly told her.

The spider climbed the table leg.

"Miss Fortune says I'm probably the best reader in the whole school," Polly said.

She gobbled her bangers and mash.

"Aaaggghhh!" she screamed.

The big, fat, hairy, scary spider was crawling over her sausage.

Polly threw her fork down. "It's that SPIDER!" she shouted.

Mr Reaper the Headmaster stood up. "What's the matter, Polly?" he asked.

"It's Yuck, Sir! It's his scary spider!"

Yuck ran over. "It's only trying to be friendly, Sir."

"I hate spiders!" Polly said.

The spider scurried across the table.

The Reaper picked up an empty glass and turned it upside down. "Gotcha!" he said, trapping the spider with it.

He took a piece of paper from his pocket and slipped it under the glass. "Yuck, come to my office immediately!"

The Reaper picked up the glass with the spider in it, and carried it to his office.

"You must not bring spiders to school, Yuck," the Reaper said.

"But, Sir! I didn't."

"Don't lie, Yuck."

"I didn't, Sir. It crawled into my bag. It's not dangerous. It's a friendly spider."

The Reaper put the glass on the shelf behind his desk. The scary spider was still

 trapped inside. It was trying to get out.

"Aren't you going to let it go, Sir?" Yuck asked.

The Reaper grinned. "I hate spiders," he said.

He handed Yuck a pile of paper. "For your punishment, I want you to write one HUNDRED lines: *I must not bring spiders to school.*"

"But, Sir—"

The Reaper booted Yuck out of his office.

That evening, Polly told Mum what had happened.

"Yuck took that spider to school!" she said. "Mr Reaper's given him lines."

Mum sent Yuck to his room to do his punishment. But all Yuck could think about was the spider trapped under the glass.

He had to rescue it, but he needed some friends to help him.

Yuck opened the door to his wardrobe and looked inside. "We have an emergency," he said.

In the darkness, crawling among the cobwebs, was his Secret Army of Spiders, the S.A.S.

Left Left Left Left
Right Right Right Right

There were Micro Spiders and Gorilla Spiders, Crane Spiders and Telescope Spiders. They were spinning parachutes, crawling up and down silk ropes, and jumping from coat hangers.

At the bottom of the wardrobe, spiders were marching eight legs at a time – left, left, left, left, right, right, right, right!

"General, are you there?" Yuck asked.

From the back of the cupboard, through a tangle of cobwebs, hobbled General Household Spider, the oldest spider in Yuck's collection.

He had one leg missing and carried a walking stick.

"I have a mission for the S.A.S.," Yuck said. "A rescue mission. It's going to take place tomorrow lunchtime at school."

Yuck told General Household Spider his plan...

The next morning, Yuck held tightly to his bag. The S.A.S. were hiding inside it.

When he arrived at school, the Reaper was waiting for him. He grabbed Yuck by the ear. "Have you done your lines, Yuck?"

"Er… a dog ate them, Sir," Yuck said.

"What dog?"

"They blew away in a whirlwind, Sir."

"Nonsense!"

"I was kidnapped by aliens, Sir."

"Come with me, Yuck!"

The Reaper dragged Yuck to his office, and handed him another bundle of paper.

"For your punishment, I want you to write ONE THOUSAND lines: *I must not bring spiders to school.*"

"One THOUSAND, Sir?"

"You're to do them in the library at lunchtime!"

"But, Sir, I can't. I'm busy this lunchtime."

"Tough," the Reaper said. "And I'll be checking up on you, so you'd better be there."

Yuck looked at the scary spider trapped under the glass on the Reaper's shelf.

It wasn't moving.

That lunchtime, Yuck called a secret meeting in the playground. Fartin Martin, Tom Bum and Little Eric gathered round. Yuck showed them the huge bundle of paper that the Reaper had given him.

"I have to stay in the library," he said.

Then he showed them the spiders in his bag.

Fartin Martin, Tom Bum and Little Eric all agreed to help.

"We'll have to work quickly," Yuck said.

Yuck raced off to the library while Little Eric ran to the art room and grabbed a pot of paint. Little Eric threw it out of the window to Tom Bum. Tom Bum rolled it across the playground to Fartin Martin. Fartin Martin passed the pot of paint through the library window to Yuck, who was waiting inside.

"Nice one," Yuck said. "Stay there until I give the signal."

Yuck grabbed the bundle of paper and spread the pages over the floor. He opened the pot of paint and unzipped his bag.

General Household Spider crawled out, followed by his troops.

"We have a minor delay," Yuck told them. He began writing: *I must not bring spiders to school.*

"Copy me," he said, pointing to the paint pot. The spiders scurried over and dipped their legs in the paint. They crawled out onto the paper scribbling, eight legs at a time...

I must not bring spiders b
I must not bring spiders b
I must not bring
I must not bring
I must not bring
I must not bring spiders b
I must not bring spiders b
I must not bring spiders b

Just then, Yuck heard the door open.

It was Polly. She'd come to get a book.

"What are YOU doing here?" she asked.

"My lines," Yuck said.

Polly looked at the sheets of paper on the floor. They were crawling with spiders.

"Aaarrrggghhh!" she screamed.

She turned and ran out of the library.

When she was gone, General Household Spider tapped Yuck's foot with his stick.

All Yuck's lines were written.

"Thank you," Yuck said.

He ran to the library window and General Household Spider followed with his troops.

Fartin Martin and Tom Bum were waiting outside.

"Are you ready?" Yuck asked them.

"All clear," they replied.

"Good luck."

The S.A.S. crawled out, and Fartin Martin and Tom Bum led the spiders along the side of the building to the Reaper's office. They peered through the window.

The Reaper was polishing a photograph of himself.

"Over there," Fartin Martin whispered.

"Under the glass," Tom Bum said.

General Household Spider crawled up to the windowsill and looked in. The scary spider was on the shelf behind the Reaper.

 Suddenly the office door burst open.

It was Polly.

Fartin Martin and Tom Bum listened.

"Quick, Sir, it's an emergency!" they heard. "Yuck's got spiders in the library!"

The Reaper ran out, slamming the door behind him.

"Over to you, General," Fartin Martin whispered.

General Household Spider waved his troops in through a gap at the bottom of the window. The rescue mission began.

The Telescope Spiders
went in first, lowering
themselves down to the
floor, looking out for
danger with their eight eyes.

A ninja squad of
black-backed Micro
Spiders scattered up
the walls and across
the ceiling.

A commando squad of
hairy-bottomed Gorilla
Spiders swung in on silk
threads, landing on the
shelf where the scary
spider was trapped.

An engineer squad of long-legged Crane
Spiders began building a silk rope-bridge
from the window to the shelf.

Tom Bum looked at the clock on the Reaper's wall. The S.A.S. would have to complete the rescue before the headmaster returned.

Fartin Martin ran back to the library window. "He's coming," he whispered to Yuck. "Good luck."

Yuck picked up the sheets of paper from the library floor and sat down at the table in the corner, pretending to write.

The Reaper opened the library door. "Where are they?" he demanded.

"Where are what, Sir?" Yuck asked.

"The spiders," Polly said, running in behind the Reaper.

"I don't know what you're talking about," Yuck said.

He stood up and handed the Reaper the big stack of paper.

The Reaper stared at the pages. He saw
the lines in tiny handwriting.

I must not bring spiders to school.
I must not bring spiders to school.
I must not bring spiders to school.
I must not bring spiders to school.
I must not bring spiders to school...

"There's a THOUSAND there," Yuck
said. "You can count them if you want."

"That was fast," the Reaper said.

"I've been working
hard all lunchtime,
Sir. There are no
spiders in here."

The Reaper
scrunched up
the bundle
of paper and
walked out
of the library.

"He's lying,
Sir," Polly said,
running after
the headmaster.

Meanwhile, Fartin Martin and Tom Bum watched through the window as the S.A.S. set to work in the Reaper's office.

The Telescope Spiders kept a lookout under the door as General Household Spider directed each squad into position.

The Micro Spiders lowered silk threads from the ceiling. The Gorilla Spiders attached the threads to the glass. The Crane Spiders secured the silk rope-bridge.

General Household Spider pointed his stick and gave the signal to begin.

The Micro Spiders pulled their threads and lifted the glass. The Gorilla Spiders dashed underneath the glass and dragged the scary spider out. It was weak and could hardly move. The Crane Spiders rushed across the bridge carrying a silk stretcher.

Just then, the Telescope Spiders signalled from the door that someone was coming. General Household Spider pointed his stick to the window and the S.A.S. moved out.

The Micro Spiders let down their threads and lowered the glass back into place. The Gorilla Spiders lifted the scary spider onto the stretcher and the Crane Spiders carried it across the rope-bridge. They all pulled the bridge up and left through the window.

Fartin Martin and Tom Bum cheered.

The S.A.S. had done it! The scary spider was saved!

Yuck was leaning out of the library window.

"Mission accomplished," Fartin Martin called to him. He ran over and handed Yuck the scary spider. "See you in a minute," he said.

The scary spider was beginning to move again. Yuck carefully placed it in his pocket, and the S.A.S crawled back into his bag. Yuck smiled and ran out of the library door.

Little Eric was waiting for him in the corridor. "Let's go," he said.

Everyone was heading to class.

Yuck and Little Eric ran down the corridor and watched as the Reaper opened the door to his office.

Polly was with him. "Yuck has got spiders, Sir. I saw them," she said.

"It's gone!" the Reaper shouted.

"What's gone, Sir?" Polly asked.

"The scary spider!"

Yuck and Little Eric were giggling in the corridor.

"Yuck!" the Reaper called.

"Yes, Sir? Is something the matter?"

"Did you take that scary spider from my office?"

"Me, Sir? I've been in the library all lunchtime, Sir."

Fartin Martin and Tom Bum came running down the corridor.

"Maybe it escaped, Sir," Fartin Martin said, giggling.

"Escaped?"

"A scary spider's on the loose!" Tom Bum said.

"A scary poisonous spider!" Little Eric said.

"A scary poisonous man-eating spider!" Yuck said.

Everyone in the corridor began running.

"There's a scary spider on the loose!"
they screamed.

"No, there isn't. It's Yuck mucking
about!" Polly shouted.

"Everyone go to your
classrooms!" the Reaper told
them. "If you see a spider, tell
me at once!"

The Reaper picked up the
glass and went on the hunt.

"Just you wait, Yuck," Polly said. "You're going to be in BIG TROUBLE."

Yuck giggled as he went into class.

"It's Polly who's going to be in BIG TROUBLE," he said to his friends.

That night, Yuck opened his bag and let all the spiders run around in his room.

The scary spider was weak. It climbed up onto Yuck's bed and he stroked it better.

"There, there," he said. "How could Polly and the Reaper be so nasty? You're not really scary."

The scary spider tickled Yuck's finger.

"Tomorrow we're going to teach the Reaper a lesson. And Polly too. We're going to set a trap," he said.

"General," he called.

General Household Spider hobbled over on his stick, and Yuck whispered his plan.

The General gathered his troops.

That night, while Mum, Dad and Polly were asleep, the S.A.S. began spinning, metre after metre of triple-thick, super-strong silk thread.

They built a huge web the size of Yuck's carpet.

Carefully, Yuck rolled it up and packed it in his school bag.

General Household Spider gave the
signal and the S.A.S. scurried out of
Yuck's door.

Yuck followed them to Polly's room.

Polly was asleep.

The spiders scurried across
her bedroom floor, up the leg
of her bed and over her duvet.

General Household Spider went first. He
hobbled over Polly's ear and crawled across
her face. He stood on her nose, peering into
her mouth.

Polly's mouth was open. She was snoring.

"Good luck, General," Yuck whispered.
"See you tomorrow."

General Household Spider waved
his stick.

He jumped into Polly's mouth.

One by one, the S.A.S. followed. Spider
after spider crawled over Polly's face and
jumped into her mouth.

Last of all, the big, fat, hairy scary spider
crawled onto Polly's
chin. It waved to
Yuck, then squeezed
in with everyone
else. With one leg
poking up, it tickled Polly's lips.

Polly's mouth closed.

Yuck giggled and crept out.

In the morning, when Yuck woke up,
Polly was standing in the doorway to his
room. She was hiccuping.

"Where are they… HIC?" she asked.

"Where are what?" Yuck giggled.

"Your spiders!"

"I don't know what you're talking about,
Polly," Yuck said.

Polly picked up the
*SPIDERS* book by his
bed. "I know you've…
HIC… been taking
spiders to school. When
the Reaper finds them
you're going to be in…
HIC… BIG TROUBLE."

Polly stormed out and Yuck giggled.

"Get up, Yuck!" Mum called.

Yuck got dressed and left for school
with Polly.

When they arrived, Polly went straight
to the library to choose an extra book
before class.

Yuck ran to the playground.

Fartin Martin, Tom Bum and Little Eric were waiting for him. He gave them the rolled-up spider's web from his bag.

"Quick, Polly's getting a book," he said.

Fartin Martin, Tom Bum and Little Eric raced off to the library.

Meanwhile, Yuck went to find the Reaper. He was at the edge of the playground, searching in the bushes.

"Have you found that scary spider, Sir?" Yuck asked.

"Not yet, but I will," the Reaper told him. He was clutching the empty glass.

"I'll help you," Yuck said.

Outside the library, Little Eric waited
in the corridor, checking that no one
was coming.

Quietly, Fartin Martin opened the
library door.

Tom Bum unrolled
the giant spiders' web.

He stood on Fartin
Martin's shoulders
and pinned it up.
Fartin Martin held
him steady as he
stretched it across
the doorway.

Inside, Polly was choosing a book from the shelf marked P.

Fartin Martin gave the signal that everything was ready, and Little Eric raced outside.

He ran across the playground to the Reaper. "Quick, Sir!" he said. "Polly's got spiders in the library!"

"Polly?" the Reaper asked.

Behind the Reaper's back, Yuck gave the thumbs up.

"Yes, Sir – lots of them," Little Eric said. "Quick, Sir, run!"

The Reaper ran as fast as he could across the playground and down the corridor to the library.

"Is the trap set?" Yuck asked Little Eric.

"Everything's ready," Little Eric said.

They ran to watch.

"Sir! What's happened?" Polly asked, turning round.

The Reaper was stuck in the web!

"Get me out of here!" he shouted.

The Reaper wriggled and struggled.

"Are you all right, Sir?" Polly asked.

"It's your spiders!" the Reaper said.

"But I haven't got any spiders. I hate spi… HIC."

Polly hiccupped and General Household Spider crawled out of her mouth.

"Aaagghh!" she screamed.

General Household Spider hobbled up to the web, and crawled onto the Reaper.

"Get it off me!" the Reaper cried.

He was trapped.

Yuck, Fartin Martin, Tom Bum
and Little Eric were standing in the
corridor, giggling.

"What's happening?" Yuck asked.

"...HIC." A Gorilla Spider swung out of
Polly's mouth on a silk thread and landed
on the Reaper.

"...HIC ...HIC ...HIC!" A long line of
spiders marched out of Polly's mouth – left,
left, left, left, right, right, right, right!

"AAAGGGHHH!" the Reaper shouted, as they scurried onto the web, crawling up and down his arms and legs, inside his shirt and over his face. They ran up his trousers and into his ears.

"Get them off me!" the Reaper begged.
"I hate spiders!"

Polly burped and the big, fat, hairy scary
spider popped out of her mouth.

Yuck peered through the web.

"There it is, Sir," he said, laughing. "It's not me who's been bringing spiders to school. It's Polly!"

Become a member of Yuck's fanclub at:
WWW.YUCKWEB.COM
Find Matt and Dave's rotten jokes, gross facts and
disgusting downloads, as well as crazy competitions
AND the first word on Yuck's new adventures.
Be warned: it's really Yucky!